A Quarantine Love Story

Namaskar, Adaab and my salaam to all of you and my name is Mohammad Zeeshan and today and now I am going to me that my first novel by the way you must have seen the cover page of this book as to what

Mohd Zeeshan

ISBN 978-93-5559-124-1
© Mohd Zeeshan 2021
Published in India 2021 by Pencil

A brand of
One Point Six Technologies Pvt. Ltd.
123, Building J2, Shram Seva Premises,
Wadala Truck Terminal, Wadala (E)
Mumbai 400037, Maharashtra, INDIA
E connect@thepencilapp.com
W www.thepencilapp.com

Author biography

Introduction of Author

Namaskar, Adaab and my salaam to all of you and my name is Mohammad Zeeshan and today and now I am going to me that my first novel by the way you must have seen the cover page of this book as to what the name of this book is even if you don't see it. Here I will tell you all the name of this novel is "A Quarantine Love Story"" That's what you're going to publish soon and soon you'll all get to read what you'll be able to connect with yourself and feel every word of it, as well as I hope you all read the way you all loved my first books. Yes, I've written more books before this. I know those who have studied, but I want to tell those who have not read them today and now that I have written four more books before which are like this "Sukoon-e-Dil", Tanhai, Chai and last one is Musafir Anjaan Rahon ka" you can all read these books on google play store all of you will get to read for free.

Now let's talk about this book what is in this Book and why should you read so I want tell you that as I have already told you that it is a Novel so you all must have knowledge about Novels yes, you're thinking right stories, yes similarly, you will get to read stories in this book also.

That's why I have a one reason I have given name this book this that name is A Quarantine Love Story the whole story based on the time when the corona virus was going on all over in the world and there were many victims in it quarantine, I hope that just as I have liked the rest of the other's books and they have been loved a lot by all of you, so you will like this book very well. You will get in this Novel to read some long and Short Story those all Stories are Fictions and Non- Fictions and much more.

CONTENTS

Epigraph

MOHAMMED ZEESHAN

Hello everyone my name is Mohammed Zeeshan and I would like to say thanks to all peoples who helped me know I would like to say thank you to my mom who gave me birth and teach me lot of ethics she is uneducated but taught me lessons of life.

My mother is world best mother even I respect every mother so every mom is the best for her children's.

Now I would like to say to all people who encouraged and helped me, Let's start with my friend Mohd Aarif Khan who recognised my ability and courage me when I was regret about few things...

If I talk about another one person that is my respected teacher Mr. Mohd Kamal Akhtar sir, I got inspiration from him and started writing more,

Now I would like enlightened name of my 2nd teacher "Leena Verma" mam she is very supportive n helpful person. She has helped me a lot in writing she corrects me

Everywhere while writing I'm wordless when I admire you ma'am thank you so much...

I'm grateful to my family and friends for their support n those who could not help me because of some reason so it ok and thanks from my side for their efforts,

I'm sorry who's name I have not mention but you all are in my heart n playing vital role. thanks to all once again.

Foreword

The published write-ups are the original contents written by the author and the contents of the respective from author side and his efforts have done his best to edit and make it free from plagiarism.The success and final outcomes of this book required a lot of guidance and assistance from the many peoples and I'm extremely privileged to have got this all along the completion of my book. All that I have done is only due to such supervision and assistance and I would not forget thank them, Lastly, I would like to thank my all friends, relatives, teachers and others peoples also whose love and guidance are with me in whatever I pursue.

Preface

Disclaimer

Hello everyone, my name is Mohammed Zeeshan and I am going to tell you about this book. The book neither promotes any casteism,

religion, gender nor violates someone's rights if anything written in this book hurts the feelings or emotion of someone living in a society so

I apologize from the bottom of my heart.

Acknowledgements

Acknowledgement

The published write-ups are the original contents written by the author and the contents of the respective from author side and

his efforts have done his best to edit and make it free from plagiarism.

The success and final outcomes of this book required a lot of guidance and assistance from the many peoples and I'm

extremely privileged to have got this all along the completion of my book. All that I have done is only due to such supervision and

assistance and I would not forget thank them,Lastly, I would like to thank my all friends, relatives, teachers and others peoples also

whose love and guidance are with me in whatever I pursue.

Me and my father

1. Me and my father

I bought the saxophone last year in October. It was a gift for my father but my father wasn't in Bengaluru. He was in Dhanbad at that time. So, I decided I'd take it with me whenever I visit home. next. Little did I know it'd take me a year before I met him.

My father sings and plays over a dozen instruments. During the 2020 lockdown, when it prevented him from meeting his jamming friends, he started recording songs on the singing app Smile. Because of multiple retakes on the app, his throat got a bit fatigued and his voice became troubled. Doctor advised him to give singing rest for a few months. It was heart-breaking for him (and us). We were habituated to begin our day with the constant hum of his ghazals in the background. But little could deter a man as gifted as him. It was at that time when father started playing the pianica (also called melodica), a tiny accordion-like reed instrument where you blow air with a pipe. Being a dextrous harmonium player, pianica was a child's play for him but he itched for more. Very cutely, one day, he said the pianica doesn't go with his personality. He's tall and broad and the pianica is tiny. It looks frivolous. I asked him what would go with his personality and he had a readymade answer: a saxophone. Really? Then he showed me videos on his Facebook. He had subscribed to a sax player and would watch his videos-mostly covers of retro Bollywood hits, day and night.

When the lockdown opened, in July 2020, I sneaked my father out to Kadence, a celebrated musical store in Koramangala, Bengaluru. We checked the costliest saxophone, the black and golden one, and my father held onto it like a child, unwilling to let go. It was for €37,000.

I looked at my father and hinted, no, Mother would get so angry at the extravaganza if we shopped this right now. We had just bought a treadmill. Thankfully, the fear of mother prevailed and we returned empty-handed. I promised my father I'd buy this when I get a salary hike, which happened in October 2020. Your Quote had just won an app challenge by the Government of India and also had got through Combinator. The black and golden saxophone was the first thing I bought from the raise.

I kept the saxophone a secret for almost a year, hoping to surprise my father whenever either of us visited each other. The instrument remained mostly packed and ate dust, apart from my initial tries when I found it terribly difficult and gave up too soon. It was soon after this that I planned to move to Himachal and then go visit my parents in Dhanbad. I decided to take the saxophone with me. I shot a video of Happy Birthday and did the grand unveiling of the surprise gift on my father's 63rd birthday on 11th August. He was so enthralled that he wanted to come sees me in Himachal for the sax, not me nor the mountains, which happened in October -exactly a year since I bought it. I tried learning and playing it in Himachal but things barely progressed. Because of the improper breath technique and the gazillion keys that exist for each minor note, it was very different from the flute which I played. I ran out of breath most of the time, of enthusiasm rest of the time. Until my parents

arrived. My father's eyes lit up upon seeing the instrument and he couldn't wait to get started.

The moment my father arrived in front of me, I surprised myself. I picked up this instrument so fast that he was taken aback. So was 1. In just three weeks, I now can play any song on it in one go. All notes opened up to me as if it were waiting for the rightful owner, my father, to arrive first. The breathing technique perfected itself and I can now play non-stop for hours much to the annoyance of my parents. My father tried playing it and almost immediately, he could pick songs on it, though he's running out of breath like I used to earlier. Yesterday, I was telling my father how I picked up so fast because I know, if I play well, he will compliment me and his compliment means the world to me. I realised why I picked the flute, harmonica, synthesizer, guitar real quick growing up. He was perpetually there to cheerlead me.

"I need an audience to learn," I exclaimed to my father with a big,

grin on my face.

To this, he had just two lines to say: "And I need solitude. It should have been me who went to Himachal with the sax."

Often, the love one has for something isn't defined by how one feels while parting with it, but while uniting after parting.

From 2007 to 2011, when I came to Delhi to study, when anyone asked for my home, I'd say Dhanbad, Jharkhand. It was where I spent my high school years, where my parents lived, where I headed back during internship-free vacations.

Then I graduated and rented a place in Safdarjung Enclave in Delhi. This became my home for the time during my one-year-long India journey. This was where I itched to come back when I got free or tired from my solo travel. For good six years, from 2011 to 2017, Delhi remained the home for my nomadic heart. No matter if I was in Paris for six months in 2014 or if I lived in Sonipat at the five-star campus of Ashoka University and in Burau (where I'm right now) in 2016 where we went to build Your Quote, my Delhi house was where I felt at peace, at home.

In 2017, disillusioned with Delhi because of no luck with funding for Your Quote, I went for greener pastures and cleaner air to Bengaluru. This is where Ashish and I raised funds and set-up our company, hiring a small team of teammates from within the YQ community.

I hated Bengaluru at first. I was exasperated to be surrounded by mostly tech and start-up folks. I missed the literary and journalistic circle of Delhi that I had. So much so that for good 3 years, I only dated people from Delhi. To have an emotional connection back to the capital. But soon, with the advent of Modi-Shah, the capital lost its sheen and felt to be on the path to the ruins, with both NCERT and the politicians rewriting the city's glorious history.

Slowly, Bengaluru became more likeable. I made new friends, found family in my teammates and new passions for running, cycling, gardening and cooking. I realised how conducive is Bengaluru for running, cycling and swimming. How, because of its clogged-up traffic, every locality has developed a hyperlocal ecosystem of facilities. Every locality has nearby parks, tennis courts, swimming pools and skating rinks. Good schools too. Perfect city to settle and raise a family. It helped me raise my family of teammates. I even tried to date in Bengaluru but it barely lasted beyond a couple of months. I missed Delhi's appetite for risks and blithe in Bengaluru folks, includes both the dates and investors.

Bengaluru stopped feeling like home during this year's lockdown, when I was alone, plump, hating myself, swigging at home 24x7. Two friends left the city and it created a void in me. The appalling side of Bengaluru was suddenly in front of my eyes. One that's corporate, too settled, almost in a coma of dreamlessness & recklessness. I tried to fill my unhappiness with Hinge dates but I was emotionally unavailable.

One shouldn't date when unhappy, it's said. I did precisely that, becoming a magnet to other unhappy folks. None healed, other than being fillers of time for each other. It was unsustainable. Unhappiness was compounding. I was eager to break away, break free.

Thus, I came to Burau, a small village in Manali, this August. It's been a month and a half here. I had been here before, once in 2012 as a traveller on way to Leh, once in 2016 as an entrepreneur with Ashish to build Your Quote, once in 2019 with my entire team as a pilgrimage to the holy birthplace of Your Quote. But this time was different. I came here alone. After the first two infatuated days with the mountains, I felt incredibly lonely. I called friends I had not spoken to in a while, spoke for long hours. I cribbed. My unhappiness changed its form but it was not gone. Burau didn't feel like home. Neither did Bengaluru nor did Delhi or Dhanbad.

I felt homeless here. I tried to go on dating apps but thankfully, there was barely anyone around. The place is so remote that it shows nobody in 5-kilometre distance, my dealbreaker distance: my years of long-distance disasters have helped me come up with this maxim-don't date someone who lives beyond a 5k run away. It won't work. I won't have the motivation to meet if they can't be a part of my daily runs. It would have been a disaster to not deal with my loneliness on my own here and once again, try to fill in with random strangers.

So, slowly, alone, I started working on myself. I started fasting regularly, working out in the morning and running in the evening. My health improved, my happiness level elevated and I started collaborating with friends who were planning on coming to the mountains. I signed up for new things. Like treks. Or bike journeys. It made me welcoming.

To friends who wanted a getaway and needed a place to stay in the mountains, I became a host, a traveller, a local tour guide. But I didn't yet know if Burau started to feel home. Not until yesterday.

I went for Hamta Pass trek with a group of 22 people. I was excited to spend 5 days away from the phone and in the midst of the mountains, but due to bad weather, our trek got cut short to 3 days. Yesterday night, after a good six hour descend, we reached Manali at 11 pm. Broken to the bones, exhausted to the point of dropping down, I had the choice to rent a hotel room for the night for a thousand rupees and just crash. But a part of me wanted the comfort of the very bed where I put my head to sleep every night for the past one and a half months. It was at that moment, I felt I wasn't homeless. I chose to instead pay a thousand rupees to a Sumo driver in the middle of the night and got dropped off at the guesthouse where I'm staying.

I didn't miss Burau while leaving for the trek. Nor did I miss it during the trek. It was only upon reaching here that I felt what this place meant to me. When I opened the door to my room & witnessed the inviting mess that my bed was, I found what home means. Home is where you want to put your head to sleep. Home is what you don't mind walking an extra mile for, even when it's hurting.

Often the love one has for something isn't measured by how one feels while parting with it but while uniting after parting.

Just returned from an incomplete 6-day Hamta Pass trek that got shortened by 3 days because of incessant rains, the worst weather in 26 years according to a local trek leader. We had to cross rivers instead of streams, face waterfalls instead of a shower, and swamps of muds instead of soil.

It rained so heavily that our tents and sleeping bags became completely soaked and we had to sleep all wet at 5°C through the night of thunder and rain. For the first time in life, I considered how incredibly lucky and privileged I am to have a dry bed and a blanket at night with me for the past 32 years. A bag full of drenched clothes and toilet papers couldn't have lasted us for even an extra day so two groups, one day apart, returned in a train of 45 people one after the other through the night.

Thank God, we were in the able hands of @indiahikes who led the pack with the dexterity of a local and the care of a professional. India hikes practises this beautiful culture and generous gesture where if you go for one trek with them, the cost of the second time you're going to the same trek is on the house. They truly want the world to trek and are best and safest at what you do. I have planned to go for this again in June next year or the year after. When it doesn't rain.

While it was an adventure for a lifetime, with night trek through the jungle and bridges while returning and rope crossing through the rivers, it is going to remain as a tiresome memory.

Magic A Ganesh Chaturthi Special Story

Magic A Ganesh Chaturthi Special Story

I remember the awe I felt when I first saw that Ganeshji at the counter. I couldn't take my eyes off him. He was the size of my nine-year-old face, rectangular, black in colour with a long tapering trunk. Perfectly sculpted body, flat back. I could even imagine where would be his home. The side of my table, just next to the pen stand. I remembered what Dadi had once said. That it was Ganeshji, not Maharishi Veda Vyas, who had written the Mahabharata. How about him finishing my homework now?

I ran up to Ma and tugged at her dupatta. She was with a friend of hers, Nina aunty, our neighbour. The two of them were going for the fair and I hinged along, like a tail.

"Ma, I found a beautiful Ganeshji, please get it for me...please."

Ma ignored my pleas, like always. She mumbled a no later, unwilling to spend money on needless things. Nina aunty, who was quite rich by the way she had a Maruti Esteem in the 90s, got curious however.

"What is it?" she asked. "A beautiful statue of Ganeshji."
"Where is it?"

I was too excited and I dragged Nina aunty by her dupatta.
Ma, helpless in front

of a richer neighbour, followed rolling her eyes.

I wagged my index finger at the statue,

howling with excitement. Isn't it beautiful

"Wow, it is. How much is this for?" Nina aunty asked the shopkeeper. "200 rupees."

"Get it packed!" she ordered. For once, I was excited for I thought it was for me. A gift from the generous rich neighbour. Ma also looked at me reassuringly, when Nina aunty said, "Didi, aap bhi le lijie ek." Didi, you too buy one. When my Ma asked the shopkeeper to pack another one, shopkeeper made a sorry face. Apparently, the one that I first spotted, the one that Nina aunty first bought was the only piece available. It was no more ours, unless Nina aunty had an ounce of heart. She hadn't.

For the rest of the journey on the rickshaw, my eyes were half-wet, as I kept peering time and again at the brown paper which Ganeshji was wrapped in, dangling inside the white polythene that hung on aunty's finger as if a hook. I wanted to steal it from her. Alas, it wasn't happening as long as my mother clenched my arms, aware of my anguish.

The moment we reached home, I ran inside and just shoved my face against my father's tummy. The sobs came a few seconds later. Loud wails, as if someone had beaten the shit out of me. I was croaking, "She stole it from me. It was mine." Papa was alarmed. He had never seen me as miserable before. He asked Ma what had transpired. She related. He asked Ma to go to the neighbouring house and borrow the Ganeshji statue just for a little while. The confused Ma did as request. Meanwhile, Papa picked me up in his arms, wiped my tears and said, "Let me take you on a long drive."

Ten minutes later, we were at a hardware shop in Nala Road in Patna, weighing a kilogram of putty. Sticky, light brown clay. He handed the packet to me and asked me to hold it tight as he drove his rickety Bajaj scooter. I did, so tight that this time no Nina aunty would be able to extricate it from my clasp. We reached home faster than usual. My father had never driven so fast before.

The next moment, he was seated on the ground opposite Nina aunty's Ganeshji (which Ma had arranged by then). He was holding the lump of clay in his hand, stamping it against the ground. It formed Ganeshji back. He asked for a spoon and a knife. Five etches later, the trunk was formed. His fingers knew addition and subtraction. He took out excess clay from the ears and shoved it to the torso. Before I could imagine, it turned into the bulging tummy of the idol. Next, the spoon scooped out excess clay from the crevices, limbs coming to surface all of a sudden, leaving a well-built Ganeshji in front of me. I was speechless, as Papa picked the excess clay littered here and there on ground and added what's been missing in Nina aunty's purchase. Moosh. The rat, Ganeshji's

vehicle.

15 minutes, we were done. I had a replica with me. A better one than the original. My tears were history and I

could not stop smiling. I had seen magic first-hand. It was the most heroic act ever performed in front of my eyes, without an ounce of macho-ness. Speechless, I watched my father paint the clay black with carpentry brushes after it dried up. He looked at me, smiled and asked me to return Nina aunty's Ganeshji before she got bothered. I nodded, unwilling to move, to let go of the trance I was in.

"By the time you return, it'd be dry and ready for your study table," my father broke my spell. "Go fast, hold carefully."

I did as ask. Holding and accepting Nina aunty's rightful purchase, I walked with grace this time. I didn't crave for it anymore. I did not need it. Not because I now had my own Ganeshji, but because I was the Ganeshji, created by the very Shiva who was sitting cross-legged in front of me in his banyan, varnishing the painted clay.

How Krishna Saved

Two months ago, an investor approached us and offered us a million dollars to start something new, and to shut down Their logic was nobody was going to invest in because there aren't as many writers to make it a billion-dollar business. We tried to contest their claim saying doesn't cater to users that are writers already but everyone. It makes people who never write before write. has 3 million writers out of 5 million, and India doesn't have that many writers, so clearly, we manufacture writers out of common people. Investor wasn't convinced and we as founders were in a dilemma.

It was a moral crisis. On one side, there was a million dollars to suitably compensate my team and ourselves after having worked at salaries much less than market value for 5 years. On other side, there were 125 million posts on which would go missing if we shut. One side was greed and a motive driven by self above company, and the other side was responsibility and the fundamental belief that we carry: company over self. But just morals weren't enough. Reality started to hit us. Suddenly, with the free credits lapsed, there was a huge overhead of server costs that we couldn't have afforded with the little revenue we were making. The investor wanted us to move to Delhi and start working on a new idea from their office starting September. They were aggressively following us.

It was at this time the Bhagwat Gita helped us. Krishna talks about dharma of a warrior is to win the war even if it means sacrificing your own. As a CEO, my dharma is to keep the company alive. This dharma gave me moral justification to let go 75% of our team during the earlier such funding crisis, but with empathy-taking care of them until they got placed, to shut the office and be 100% remote and now, to call for help from our writers when we lack the wherewithal to fight back with our little army of 10. In a fit of guilt and hope, one evening during my walk in Himachal, I wrote back to the investor: "Thank you for your belief in us. But I don't think we are ready to shut down. We owe it to our writers, we can't let go of 125 million posts of theirs, their history documented in words. We will go to our writers for funds. If we can take a stand for our writers, they can take a stand for us. The community will keep alive."

Running is like running a country's government for us. We have our own constitution, our own values which embody the pillars of democracy, liberalism, secularism. We don't differentiate between religions, language, regions, caste, creed and colour. Our law and order are constantly deploying technology against anything that makes any citizen of feel unsafe or harassed. A good democracy functions when the citizens uphold the constitution and the leaders are open to feedback and criticism. Our email mz5828359@gmail.com responds to every query within 6 hours and I'm personally accessible to each user alike when they have a trouble. When is home to so many users and we listen to them, we believe our users too will listen to us?

This is what gave us the faith that instead of shutting down and starting something new, let us be transparent to our family members, our writers. If means something to them, they will come forward to save it not only for themselves but also for others who can't afford Premium. We revealed our story to the community on our birthday and the kind of response we have got over the last two days has overwhelmed us. So many writers have come forward to gift premium and to help stay alive. It feels this is our great Mahabharata and Krishna and his entire army is on our side, on the side of dharma, not greed. Happy Janmashtami.

On Travel & Living -

In 2014, when I spent 5 months in Paris as an exchange student, I started questioning how the world glorified travel. I felt that the way the world, and I, saw travel was overrated. Having spent 2012-13 solo travelling across India, I found it didn't drastically alter my life. The only impact it had on me was it made me comfortable with uncertainty and the unknown, and made me more trusting of strangers which is certainly meaningful, but even entrepreneurship or skipping campus placements teach us that, so why only travel?

One major reason behind my scepticism was that as a writer, I could not imagine setting any of my stories in any place I briefly visited. None of my short fiction could be set in Rome or Amsterdam or Shanghai or Colombo. I had neither the narrative landscape nor the lasting emotional hook that a place offers to set my stories. Contrast it with the cities I lived in Patna, Delhi, Dhanbad, Bengaluru, Manali, Hazaribagh, I could write a frigging novel set in those places and I have. In fact, Green Mango More, my last book, has stories from my schooldays in Hazaribagh. I figured that to acquaint oneself with a place as a writer, one had to live at a place for substantial time, not just travel. Hence, while the rest of my friends flocked countries after countries in Europe over weekends, I decided to spend most of my time in living Paris, in walking to Sciences Po from the 13th arrondissement, in pedalling my second-hand bike along the Seine, in sunbathing in its Jardin's and lunching at its boulangeries and museums, in being pickpocketed in the malodorous RER and in getting my heart broken. With time, Paris became a suitable backdrop for my literary works.

Over the years, people have needlessly added a spiritual connotation to travel, which is mere hogwash. Travel doesn't enlighten you. It's you who can and, if indeed, eventually does, and that can be triggered by reading, philosophising, meditating, by people or by circumstances. This was the reason I stopped doing weekend getaways, too. If I travelled, it was for people than the place because I know that spending 4 days in Ahmedabad would offer me no revealing insights about the city, however it could be insightful about the already known friend I'm travelling with/to.

Whereas travelling is exhilarating in moments, it is tiring in most parts. Travelling for travelling's sake is a chore, because the primary intention becomes sharing what you're seeing with the world see how I have been barraging my insta stories with the pics from Himachal in the past one week. Don't worry, it won't last for long. The first week I'm more of a traveller than a resident.

Give it a couple of more weeks and I'll turn as taciturn about the mountains as I was about trees in Bengaluru. Because then. instead of photos, something else will satiate my expressive heart. Writing.

My 32nd Birthday wish

Today, after a really long time, I went for an hour long run. Earlier, I'd complete almost 10k in this time but today I barely managed 5k.

Last couple of months, I have been at my unhealthiest. I got tired of cooking, of living alone in Bengaluru, of Bengaluru in general (one of the triggers that's setting me out of the city to Himachal from August). I spent the last couple of months hogging

McDonald's & Subway with only F.R.I.E.N.D.S on Netflix for

company.

The worst feeling today was when I came back home and tried to stretch. My fingers barely reached my toe when I lumbered down. The huge flab in between prevented me from touching the ground. Earlier, I could put my entire palm on the ground with my knees straight while bending down. I am at my unfit max. This Monday, after hogging McDs 3 times in a day, I peaked all time high weight of 95 kgs, eleven kgs above my BMI and I felt scared about my life. I felt I might not survive for long. It gave birth to a wish, a wish to live and no better day to fulfil this wish than the day I celebrate my birthday.

I am going to turn 32 on 29th August and I want to be able to run 32 kilometres in one stretch that day. I'd be in Himachal this time and I plan to do this run there in a mix of uphill and downhill, 16k up and 16k down. I'm going to be training for the same this month and the next. Today's 5k was a start and it was mostly brisk walk. I have already chucked sugar from my diet and regulating my rice intake henceforth. Swiggy cheat days are going to be reduced to once a week, only with friends until I'm here.

Fruits, homemade food, intermittent fasting coupled with workout, both strength and cardio, are going to be my friends the next few months. I'm also listening to this wonderful book called Beyond Training, which proposes a more holistic and humane way for endurance training. When it comes to training, less is more, is its central thesis. That is 20 minutes interval runs are better than 3 hour long runs for the longevity and overall fitness. I'll post more learnings from that too.

Inspired by my friend Anurag Maloo, who's posting about his running journeys here, I'll use as a discipline enforcer and dream documenter, posting about my journey to a better health under the hashtag

#32kms32years. Hope you'll join with me. Here is today's stat:

Balcony letter Feminist Relationship 188

Ever since I was inducted into the liberal arts, when I read the history of the feminism movement, I started to identify myself as a feminist.

It wasn't easy at first. I would get defensive, my toxic masculinity coming up to defend the mankind, chanting not-all-men-harass not realising how all-women-are-harassed. That men don't deserve sympathy for being nice when most of their not-so-nice friends are busy making the world an unsafe and unequal place. It took me a few years to strip away the misogynist conditioning that I carried from growing up in a patriarchal household and attending a sexist engineering college. After being around friends who were feminists and would correct and educate me about the inherent misogyny in my words, listening to their stories of harassment and discrimination, I was able to identify my privileges as a man and the sexist streaks within me. It helped set myself on a path of self-correction whenever something problematic came out of my mouth or pen. I thought that was enough but it wasn't. It made me a feminist individually but not in a shared space. It was not until I shared my life with you that I learnt how to be a feminist in a relationship.

Earlier, I thought feminism was this token equality. The idea of going Dutch on dates, the idea of dividing work in the household, the idea of sharing expenses equally. Being with you, I learnt that being a feminist in a relationship isn't just about equality but equity. You taught me that going Dutch on dates or sharing expenses equally is flawed when both of us earn different amounts of incomes. Instead of equally, it should be equitably divided. Soon, we started dividing our expenses in the proportion of our salaries. At that time, I was earning a lac rupee a month and you were earning sixty thousand rupees. We shared all our expenses in the 10:6 ratio. To not make it very transactional and not indulge in needless bookkeeping every night, I started opting for the costlier expense. Your costlier air ticket would be taken care by me for one way, I'd take care of stay and lodging while travelling whereas you'd pay for food.

Few months later, owing to a funding crisis, I had to lay off 75% of my team and I took a 70% pay cut. My salary reduced from 1 lac to 30 thousand rupees a month. I was shy to tell you this but you extracted it out of me. You started contributing twice as much as me in our every expense thereafter. Booking my costlier air tickets when I travelled to see you, paying twice the amount for dates and when it came to buying books, always paying for the costliest book among the stack I bought with my tiny salary.

After you, it was so difficult to be with anyone. Everyone turned out to be insecure about divulging how much they earn, to be able to make the shared living & the relationship more equitable, more feminist. I would propose paying for one way of the flight to my next partners and they'd think it was chivalrous, missing the whole feminist point. I didn't realise how difficult it would be to propose an idea as radical yet as fair and simple as equitable distribution of wealth inside the household. No wonder, for the longest time, on all the dating apps, in the "looking for" box, I wrote: a feminist.

I met many feminists in the process, all of them understood and vocalised its need and its revolutionary history, raised voice against the patriarchy and oppression, educated its theories out loud but when it came to practise, I found most shied away from it especially inside the household. After a while, I changed my "looking for" in dating apps to: a practising feminist. And then I realised I didn't need to look further. I needed to look behind. When I looked, I didn't see you behind either, but right next to me, feet to feet. Equity, in practice. That's when I stopped looking and reached out for your hand.

Balcony letter Feminist Relationship 185

I painted you a few months after you left. The only person I ever painted. Acrylic on canvas. Three colours: cobalt blue, burnt sienna and ivory black. It's an impressionistic painting of you holding the blue jacket of Olga Tokarczyk's Nobel-winning book Flights that we bought two copies of, together, a year ago. The book I shared in the balcony letter 173. Your eyes in the painting look straight in the eye of the one in front, your curly hair just the right kind of short that you like and your face as mysterious as you, half-smile, half-sorrow. You sent a heart when I had posted an Instagram story about the painting. Even your friends that followed me recognised it's you. It's my best work. Raw like me, sophisticated like you. With you gone, it was my way of having you around every day.

I pasted this painting with double sided tape behind the stack of books in my bookshelf, the stack that contained Flights. It remained stuck there for good eight months while we both remained single. It'd watch me dust, cook, walk, write, workout. Then one morning, I woke up and found it fallen behind the books. The tapes had come off.

When I first looked at it, I broke into a wide smile. In the evening, I called you to ask if you had started seeing someone. You said yes with a lot of hitches, as if I caught you red-handed with a secret. It started yesterday itself, you said. You asked me how I knew. I told you, just a feeling, telepathy maybe. I assured I was very happy to hear that. That love is a beautiful feeling and you, out of all the people in the world, deserved all the love. You thanked me, not knowing how I knew what I knew. Unlike me, you're an extremely private person and you hadn't spilled any beans about your personal life on social media or to me. Your curiosity was justified.

I cut the call and put more cello tape on the painting and fixed it back to where it was. You didn't need to evade anymore, nobody's judging, I said to you in the painting. It worked but only for a little while. No amount of cello tape was enough, soon. It kept falling from time to time, as you were falling deeper and deeper in love with the new person. Over the next year, I had figured ways, which included mixing multiple single-sided and double-sided tapes with gum, to keep the painting glued to the bookshelf wall. You were not hiding away anymore, neither the painting, nor our conversations as friends and former lovers. Fast forward one and a half years, you were falling out of love. The one you fell for wasn't ready to take a stand for you, to introduce you to his parents. You were in love but it was a love with no future. Like a writer's career.

Around the same time, in early 2021s, I started seeing someone new. Upon getting to know I had a painting of my ex peeping from behind my books, she asked me to remove it. I protested, saying it was just a painting. That my father paints and he have nude paintings stuck on the wall of our house but my mother never had problems with it because she treats art as art. This is just a portrait, my best work. She was insistent, saying she didn't want reminders of my past in her life. It was either going to be the painting, or her. That evening, I painfully took off the painting from the bookshelf. All its cello tapes undone like layers of our clothing before sleeping together once upon a time. I put the canvas in a laminated sheet, zipped the folder and put it in the almirah. Before I put it away, I had to say my ceremonious goodbye.

"This is it; this is how long you were to stay with me," I said, looking at those two understanding eyes in the painting. I texted you too, the picture of the empty bookshelf, and then after having replaced with another painting. A landscape, a sunset to be precise. The before and after. Even though I had removed the painting for this new woman, I felt like missing a part of me when with her. I was changing myself for someone else, something that I had never done, and should never have done. Something nobody should do. I could barely stand it. The absence of choice for putting a painting by me in my own home felt stifling. It felt controlling on the part of this new person. I conveyed I would want to bring the painting back, because it's a part of me and I cannot not be myself. It was inauthentic of me. She didn't understand. It led to fights, breakups and patch-ups, more breakups & more patch-ups, until eventually, it culminated into the timely departure of this new person. Forever. We were not right for each other. I felt relieved.

A week after the end, I went back to my paintings folder, took out the lamination and brought out your portrait once again with a warm hello.

"Here we go, again," I said to your portrait. I cut four slim slices of single-sided cello tape, barely one-tenth of what was needed earlier for the painting to stand its ground and pasted the canvas back on the bookshelf wall. This time, it stuck as if a tattoo, unwilling to move, unwilling to let go. You have been watching me. Dust, cook, walk, write, workout. I have been single since. You, too. We meet soon. Here we go, again.

Balcony letter 173 3rd October, 2018

We spend our day reading about a fascinating book: Flights by Olga Tokarczyk, a prizewinning novel which talks about what it means to be a traveller, a wanderer, a body in motion not only through space but through time. As you're flying tomorrow & given how badly both of us want to read this book, a novel in fragments literally a novel travelling through time, we decide that wasting even a day isn't an option. Both of us want to read & dissect it simultaneously. Hence, two copies.

Evening, I call Blossoms Bookstores after lazing for hours & they inform us that they have the book. We drive hastily, as if on a pilgrimage, leaving everything aside. The bookshop owner says he only has one copy. We are befuddled. Who gets to keep this? Letting go of our desperation, I suggest you keep it while you suggest I keep it. You, I, you, I. We aren't able to decide-after all, this wasn't the part of the plan. It's funnily poetic. How this exact journey of ours has different destinations for us both.

I tell you I will write a poem about this unexpected outcome. As we're about to leave with that one copy, the owner calls & hands over a new copy he got from the god own. The ending has changed. It's no more poetic but very fulfilling. Hence, prose.

P. S. Sundays, I post my balcony letters for free. Today's free letter made me go through all the older #balconyletters and excavate my favourite letter written for the one I have been writing about of late.

How it is to a Writer Tribes

I have eight close writer friends. They all are in different stages of their journey. A couple of them have won big prizes, like the Commonwealth Short Story Prize, one of them has a book coming out next year, one is a friend who's working on a magical realism novel and three of them are really good poets. All of them are avid readers.

If you notice me hanging out with my writer friends, we would seem like arch-enemies, ready to kill each other. We have such strong opinions on each other's writings, such strong pet-peeves about each other's writing styles and the kind of writing we all do that it'd be hard to fathom why we are friends in the first place.

My friends ridicule me for being too mushy and at times cheesy in my write-ups, most of which is around love. They criticise me for making YQ filled with writers like me. I laugh with them because there's some truth to it. I criticise some of them for being verbose & their prose being sleep-inducing as they lack wit, and some of them for being utterly talentless when it comes to storytelling being so obsessed with language that they lose the plot. They hate me for being too confident and cocky about my writing, when they believe most of my writing is very surface level. It's hard to disagree there, especially on subjects which require deeper insight than what the short form landscape of YQ offers. My confidence stems from having spent more time in pursuing writing full-time sacrificing my career, my survival for it. When you operate with a mindset where you put everything on the line, you need confidence else world will crush you. They get it too and probably that's why they stand me. Even admire me. My friends believe I'm too massy. That I am like Arundhati Roy writing for a Chetan Bhagat audience. Given I like to be read more than awarded, I don't deny their assertion.

Most of my friends are better poets than storytellers, because most

of them have had language as their starting points. They started

to read early, sentences appear in their dreams instead of story

lines that appear in mine. I started as a storyteller. As an engineer,

plots seemed logical and language became the aid to take the plot

forward than the starting point. Hence, my plots are tighter and

punchlines are kickass but language lacks meter and lyrical quality

in them that many of my friends have. I have been working on language over the years as my friends have been working on them

plots thanks to the staunch criticism we bestowed on each other.

By criticising each other, we end up respecting each other because we all know that we only have a strong opinion on stuff that we read. We are friends because each moment, we feel privileged to know we are being

read by each other.

CALLER ID A MIDDLE SCHOOL LOVE STORY

When I was in middle school, I developed a huge crush on my class

monitor Shambhavi. She was soft-spoken, studious, and happened

to be the only girl in class who spoke to me, rather reprimanded

me. She noticed me giggling during the break when everyone was

supposed to be quiet. Angry, she came up to me and said, "Shut

your mouth up otherwise I'd break your teeth." That was the first

time in middle school when a girl had talked to me. Her words

felt like honey to my ears. I abided, shut my mouth and saved me

teeth. However, I couldn't help but flash a dreamy smile at her.

My crush intensified with every passing day. I started giggling more often just to notice my name written in her delicate handwriting on the blackboard, which attracted fatal beatings from our class teacher once. I bore that. Love means sacrifice, Bollywood had taught me. Two weeks into my crush, a disaster happened. Our class teacher appointed a new class monitor, since the coveted position of responsibility seemed to affect Shambhavi's performance in class. Unsurprisingly, the new monitor was none other than me. Our visionary teacher thought making me the monitor would help tame me. It in fact did just that. I took the new role rather seriously. In my head, now, I was the right match for Shambhavi. I could imagine going to her parents someday, asking for her hand and telling how I am the best monitor class 6A ever had, second only to your daughter.

Now our roles had changed. But unlike me, Shambhavi never talked or giggled in between classes. She was way too sincere for me to scribble her name on the board in my illegible handwriting. I missed the old days. And I wanted to speak to her, to get chided by her but none of that happened. One week into my new responsibility, I could not control my desire to speak to her, but I apprehended that if I went towards the girl's row just to specifically talk to her, it would attract jabs from all my friends. Half of my male friends already knew that I liked to catch her attention. It is said that when you desperately want something, universe conspires to make it happen. And it did.

he class teacher called and asked me to count everyone's attendance over the year and report it to him. As soon as I flipped through the pages of the attendance register, my face shone with delight as if I'd found a treasure. Now I had access to all the details about each and every student in the class from address to the phone number, to even grandparents' name. Too small to think about privacy and stalking, I noted her phone number in my diary, hoping to convey my feelings over phone-in private-without any of my friends getting to know.

That evening, at home, when my mother went for an evening walk, I pursued my year long ambition. Jittery, I dialled her number, waited for a few seconds until it started ringing. Every subsequent ring pounded my heart until it became so loud that I started wobbling. Shambhavi picked up the phone, her sing-song voice uttered a series of sweet hellos in sync with my heartbeats. No matter what I'd planned, I could not mumble anything. After hearing her four to five hellos, I put the receiver of the phone down and sighed. It took me five minutes to calm myself down. My desperation to convey made me call her again, but this time, I was all prepared. The moment she picked it up, I played the song 'Humko Sirf Tumse Pyaar Hai' (I am in love with only you) on the speakers and let it play for a minute. She didn't cut the phone during this time, which hinted to me that she kind of liked the song, which I presumed to be her yes to my weird proposal. This time I was not wobbly, this time I was not nervous. The fact that she stayed on the phone all the while was the reason for my newfound confidence.

I stopped the song, a surreal silence followed when I could hear her breaths. It was the moment-the moment of claiming my crush and revealing myself. Before I could say anything, she bombarded, "Who the hell is this? I have a caller ID. I have noted this number down and now I am going to complain to the police right away."

I started shivering, beads of sweat rolled down from my head, drenching the phone receiver in it, while my body experienced a tiny earthquake. In the hour that followed after the disastrous call, all that I could imagine was police coming over to my home and arresting my father, for our landline phone belonged to his name. I lost my sanity, having no idea what to do next. Our doorbell rang just at that moment, making my heartbeats go haywire. All I could think of was a bunch of police officers with two handcuffs one small and one big-to tie up both the son and the father. Me for flirting with my school crush, him for providing me the way to do that. Accomplice father, no less! I nervously stood at the front of the shut door, heard the doorbell ring a couple of more times, and then, with utmost caution, I opened the door. I saw my father weary from office standing there, with an extremely annoyed what-took-you-so-long look on his face.

Before he could say anything, I grabbed him by his sleeves, asked him to drive both of us away to as far as he could. Before I could pester him anymore to come along with me, the phone rang. My father rushed in towards the phone. Despite my reckless cries, "Dad, don't. It must be the police," he picked the phone up. I could only sheepishly mutter to myself, "ab to gaye". He didn't listen.

"Harsh, it's for you. It's your classmate Shambhavi," my dad said a moment later, surprised at me receiving a call from a girl for the first time in my life. Embarrassed for two reasons now, I wondered whether Shambhavi figured that it was I who was on the phone that time i.e., whether she, as a monitor, had noted down my number too. Frightened and curious, I grabbed the receiver and I said a mild hello. All I could hear from the other end was the song: "Tujhe mirchi lagi to main kya karun?" (If chillies burn your tongue, why should I bother?)

The Family Tree A Short Story

Once upon a time, there lived a barber. He had a 16-year-old son, thoroughly disinterested in his father's vocation, but the barber forced him into his business right after his school. He feared that if he studied further, the son might leave him and the village and settle in the city.

His son unwillingly complied by his father's wishes and began working with him. He hated the damn job and often undertook the task callously. He preferred listening to the stories that the waiting customers gossiped about rather than cutting the hair. Within three weeks as a novice barber, he ended up injuring five of his customers, rather intentionally, to make his father observe his disinterest. His trick worked. Frightened that his mediocre son might spoil his reputation in the village, the barber forbade him from the job. He was glad and decided that from now on, he would spend his time overhearing people at the paan-shop who returned from cities, who talked about the big skyscrapers, the fancy cars, the pretty madams, and the rags to riches stories. As he got fancied into the beguiling charms of the cities more and more, he realized how much he hated the closed environment of his village and how many opportunities did the city hold for him. He tried to convince his father to allow him to go, but to no use. But he didn't give up. Every morning when his father used to go to his shop, he accompanied him and talked about how the city could help him strengthen the family's financial status. The barber, though cold initially, upon seeing his son's obstinacy, ultimately allowed him to go to the city on the condition that he would send 50 rupees per month to the family, as soon as he got settled.

The son assured his parents that he would figure out a way to earn for himself as soon as he could find a job. It was the first moment when his father felt proud to not have him join the family-occupation. The young man embarked on his journey towards everything that enamoured him during his daydreams. Upon arriving in the city, he was awed and tried to find a firm ground beneath his feet. But the life in the city was not as easy as he thought. There was cut-throat competition coupled with unemployment and high expenses; even people who had been more educated than him ran from office to office in search of jobs. The little money that he carried from home didn't last long. Unlike what he had thought, nobody hired him after realizing that he wasn't even a college graduate. Unable to pay for his expenses, for one week, he had to sleep at the railway station. He got so hopeless that he decided to go back to his village, but his self-respect forbad from breaking down. What would he tell his father? He struggled, for over six months, until he discovered his talent - a way to sustain himself in the city. One and a half year later, after not hearing from his son for as long, the barber received an envelope carrying 900 rupees with a note of thanks dedicated to him from his son, not disclosing the reason why.

Twenty years later, a prominent barber in the city is trying to induct his 16-year-old son into the profession. His son is not willing and he intentionally injures a couple of regular clients of his father. The father gives up and exempts him from work. Delighted, he spends time at a local bar where he overhears people who have returned from Dubai talk about the world's tallest skyscrapers, about the beautiful Arabian madams, the fancy limousines, and the rags to riches stories.

Balcony Letter 157

The Most Memorable Parting Gift

The most memorable parting gift I ever got from a lover was a pie-chart from you: a Pacman-like pie with two slices, drawn hurriedly on yellow paper, minutes before ending our year-long relationship. The smaller slice represented you and the giant gabby Pacman mouth was me. You said, this is how our relationship felt like. That I hogged all the airtime-on the phone, in person talking about myself, going on and on, not listening, never asking about you. That I didn't know you. You didn't feel understood.

All the while, I kept thinking it was going smooth. That you were happy with me, loved listening to me. You did. But for how long can one take a one-sided conversation? It went downhill without me knowing. I asked you, crying out loud, why didn't you tell me earlier? You showed me the pie and asked, where was the space when you never listened? This time, I did. O boy, I did! There was nothing I could disagree with. You were right and it was too late. Out of hope, out of love, I left.

I kept looking at the crumpled pie-chart in my hand all through my metro ride. How come you were able to tell me that now? Did I magically become a good listener? That's when it struck me. A lover can be the most honest with you only when they stop loving you.

Prologue

Prologue.........

18th September, 2016 Solang Valley, Himachal

It's 7 in the morning. The first rays of the sun have turned the icy tip of Hanuman Tibba red. It's the highest peak in the vicinity, standing tall at 5982 meters and from my window, it feels like one cannonball away. I watch it from my bed, lingering out of part-laziness, part-cold and part-awe. A minute later, it turns into an orange as if someone added a dash of yellow to the red.

Wrapped within two layers of blankets, I don't wish to get up but my bladder likes being a rebel to my mind. Especially in the morning. Ten minutes of watching the colours melt, I remove the blanket, grab my smartphone from the charging station and drag myself towards the loo. The temperature in the room is less than 10 degrees, the toilet rim is frigid and leaving behind the beauty of the mountains outside, I bury my head into my phone. Time for the morning ritual.

I kickstart the day by clicking the 3 bars of the one app that makes me hold my breath more than my bladder.

Google Analytics. The cold stops bothering me and my body warms up with anxiety. Would yesterday's traffic have surpassed the day before yesterdays? The daily active users on 16th were 323, it better be more! I mutter to myself as the app loads in the not-so-fast 3G of the remote Himalayas. 344. The number flashes on the screen. I let out the sigh I have been holding since before I went to sleep. It's 6.5% better than the previous day. A gift of one more day to fight and scale, another day to evade death.

For entrepreneurs who have failed 3 products in quick succession, for someone who has seen the traffic first bulge up and then fall down in each of them, every single day begins with paranoia. What if this one too ends up with the same fate as the previous three? No signs of stalling however. It's been 3 weeks since the launch of Your Quote on 28th August and every single day, the traction has grown. It started with 21 users on the first day, 25 on the second, 34 on the third and not a single day where the traffic slumped. Organically scaling. No marketing beyond the first announcement. People are coming, writing, sharing and their friends are coming, writing, sharing and their friends follow the footsteps.

I figure I have warmed the rim long enough for my cofounder, Ashish, whenever he wakes up. Keeping the phone back into the pocket, I freshen up and come out. I look towards Ashish, fast asleep on the single bed a foot away. When we arrived at the guesthouse, it was a double bed, ideal for honeymooners, but we separated it a foot apart: the only kind of privacy two straight, single men working and living together desire. His laptop is plugged in by his bedside. He must be up working till late the previous night. Deployment of new features happens only when the world is asleep so that if accidentally a bug goes live, it affects the least number of users.

The sun has dipped most of Hanuman Tibba in its yellow. It's now too glittery to watch. I walk towards the balcony next to the common kitchen. It opens into the valley. Everything is covered in mist. Sunlight hasn't yet reached the sleepy villages beside these tall mountains. Bauji, the seventy-year-old cook, is up and he's making the morning tea. For himself and me. September is an off-season and we are the only guests in this guesthouse. He greets me with a toothless grin. I stretch, do a few sit-ups and stretch my cold legs in the first rays of sun that arrive in the balcony like a shy visitor. It'll only be at eleven that the sun will light up the whole valley. Until then, it will creep in like the smell of ginger chai in the balcony.

Holding the sugary chai in my hand, I start work. Today is the last date to apply in Combinator, the world's largest start-up accelerator, the mecca for tech start-ups. Based in Silicon Valley, they have helped build companies like AirBnb, Dropbox, Quora, Reddit among others. We have applied thrice with previous products, only to get rejected. This is going to be the fourth attempt, the first with YourQuote. I am hopeful.

A quarantine Love Story

The girl at the billing counter was registering in the bought items with a bar code scanner and simultaneously making wayward side eyes at Padmanjali. Padmanjali let out a smirk knowing that the white thread stitched onto her coal black mask in the shape of a permanent smile spooked people up much more than her fake smile ever did.

As she walked back to her hostel holding onto to her bag of purchased items, she invited many more of such unsought, curious glances her way on account of her unique mask. By the time Padmanjali was back in her room, she had decided that her new mask was going to be another one of those things that she possessed which was going to stay locked up in her closet, being too quirky for the world to handle at present.

Later in the evening Padmanjali climbed up the stairs to her hostel terrace for her usual evening stroll. She had carefully planned and chosen a time after sunset when the terrace was least likely to be occupied by anyone else due to the mosquito problem; she would rather bear the mosquito bites than be in the company of a hostel mate.

As Padmanjali entered the terrace she let out of a sigh of disappointment; the whole place was filled with lines of clothes, some wet, but majority of them dried, hanging around like abandoned rows of ghosts that fluttered in the late evening breeze.

On a corner of the terrace, next to the washing stone someone had left a half-filled bucket. She could see the reflection of the moon trembling inside it in a background of pale blue sky that had yet to turn dark, giving it an ominous vibe that matched with the times. As there was hardly any space left in the terrace for her to walk, she decided to observe the people around instead.

Padmanjali had always liked to observe people from a distance, taking note of their movements, expressions, their quirks and mannerisms; it had always intrigued her how things that could be boring up close were so interesting from a distance. She was grateful to the lockdown, it had given her ready license to such questionable endeavours, with every human being on the planet turning into a 'people watcher' in their own right.

Opposite to her building she saw a lady and her teenage daughter, walking back and forth, moving their hands in wide arc-shaped motions that looked funny to her eyes. The daughter was cautiously stealing glances at a boy in the next building who was doing vigorous push-ups on the roof floor, most likely with the motive of impressing her. The grumpy disapproving face of the mother made Padmanjali smile, she would have drawn a curtain between her daughter and the boy if she could.

Padmanjali moved closer to the edge of the terrace and looked down. She could see the narrow lane next to her hostel that led to a wider road. Irrespective of whether the lockdown existed or not, the roads were brimming with people in the evening; she liked that about Bangalore, nothing could ever bring that city to a halt.

Among the crowd she spotted a familiar looking fellow walking as if he had spring in his legs; a young man living in the building next to Padmanjali's hostel. She had noticed him with interest a couple of times on account of his long shabby hair tied into a bun and because of the fact that he couldn't resist petting a dog on the way if he found one.

But the one trait that stood out the most about him was his long bony legs and today he was wearing a pair of hot pants, flaunting those slender legs in full display. There was something about chicken legs that was truly enchanting for Padmanjali, but she couldn't put a finger on the exact reason why she found it attractive in a man, she figured it had got something to do with the fact that a man with such wiry legs could neither chase her down nor run away from her side too quickly. She kept her eyes fixed on the fellow till he disappeared at the corner in the end of the lane.

After that she just observed random people buying stuff from the shop at the corner. Some of them were keeping a two-meter social distance and some just didn't care about the rule. For no particular reason Padmanjali liked to keep a mental note about the ones who did follow the rule and the ones who didn't.

Later, when the sky turned dark, she tip-toed back into her room, relieved that she didn't meet anyone on her way down stairs. Her room looked like a tiny prison cell; a bed, a table and a chair were the only furniture inside it and those occupied most of the space leaving only a tiny stretch for her to walk around. The bathroom attached to the room was so small that it could be mistaken for a wardrobe. Inspire of all this Padmanjali was really grateful for the room, a single room like this was a big luxury in a city like Bangalore, especially with her meagre salary.

Padmanjali had her dinner and went early to sleep. But even though she was lying on the bed for hours, she couldn't sleep. She woke up and decided to surf videos on her mobile instead, but she got bored of that too after some time. Later when she became too restless, she got up from up from her bed and moved towards the window near the table, the only window in her room, to take in some air.

It wasn't really much of a window to begin with as just a couple of meters away there was another building that blocked most of the light and air that entered her room. And there was a window on the next building, directly opposite to her which was always locked shut. Sometimes her window looked like a painting of another window closed shut.

At present in the dim street light, she could barely make out the brown wooden edge of the window in the opposite building. She could also sense a faint cold breeze, that had managed to squeeze in between the two buildings and caress her face.

Suddenly a thought struck Padmanjali, what if the window opposite to her opened right now? What would she find inside? Somehow that idea excited her. But that night the window remained tight shut and it would remain so for many days yet to come. But one day, a couple of months from now, things would change.

One day the window opposite to her room would open and to her astonishment Padmanjali would find that it was the boy with the chicken legs who had lived there all along. It would be the first time that she had seen him without his face mask, but she would recognise him anyway. His face would be both similar and different from the way she had imagined it. He would have had a sharp nose, a bit too sharp, giving him an air of roughness, but his mouth would be round and smooth, as if to balance off the edge.

One day the window opposite to her room would open and to her astonishment Padmanjali would find that it was the boy with the chicken legs who had lived there all along. It would be the first time that she had seen him without his face mask, but she would recognise him anyway. His face would be both similar and different from the way she had imagined it. He would have had a sharp nose, a bit too sharp, giving him an air of roughness, but his mouth would be round and smooth, as if to balance off the edge.

The boy would also give her a glance of recognition, barely lasting a second, but enough for Padmanjali to realise that he had noticed her before too, perhaps on the streets, perhaps when she was busy with evening strolls on the terrace and had been inconspicuous about the whole thing like her.

After the initial awkwardness, they would both settle down to their usual routine and Padmanjali would watch a movie in her laptop with headphones on the bed, a soft smile lining her face knowing that the window opposite to her was still open. In between she would notice the boy sitting on his chair and laughing at something in his mobile and would wonder whether he had also noticed the change in her expressions as she watched her film.

At noon Padmanjali would notice him leave the room and wonder if he had gone out to eat. Soon she would realise that she was hungry herself and would go and get some food from the canteen below. When she would come back inside her room, she would notice him sitting silently on his chair and eating. She would go straight, sit on her bed and affably eat her meals, a strange sense of warmth budding inside her at the familial scene.

In the evening when Padmanjali would go out for her walk in the terrace, she would wonder: how did she get so familiar with a stranger living next to her just a few meters away? She would start to feel a little annoyed that she had let some strange fellow have a glimpse of her private life, the way she slept, the way she ate, the way she laughed, all those little moments of solitude, now totally exposed. She would decide to just go down and shut the window to his room herself. But on the way down the stairs, she would realise that she had kind of missed him already and with a smile understand that she had already fallen hard.

When she would reach her room, it would have been half past eight already; Later that night she would play songs from her mobile playlist, a little too loud for him to hear and with palpitations she would turn to look at the window opposite to her, afraid that she might see a face crumpled with annoyance, afraid that she might hear the sound of a window slamming on her. But all she would find would be a calm face coated with a gentle smile, eyes softly shut, waving rhythmically to the song.

The next morning when Padmanjali would wake up she would notice that the boy was still asleep. Later, after she had taken a bath, hair still dripping wet, she would look at the window and he would be looking straight at her. For some time, they would hold on to each other's gaze, powerless to look away. When they finally break away, she would wave at him and he would wave back. Later she would make a sign with her hands as if asking him to wait for a second, when she would be back again, she would have the black mask in her hands, the one stitched with the smile. She would put it on her face with trembling hands and look at him. He would move away from the window and for a second Padmanjali would feel that her heart had been crushed with the weight of the world. But he would return soon, just a few moments later, wearing a black mask himself, a surprise stitched on it with a white thread in the shape of an 'O'. Padmanjali would laugh in relief and for a while a genuine smile would bloom on her face underneath her a black smiley mask.

Author's note: Initially I thought of writing this story in parts, mostly because I was going through a creative block and a daunting day job and I thought that writing in parts might help. But somehow the story looks chopped up because of that. So, I published it as a single piece now. I am sorry for the inconvenience caused to those who have already read the first two parts.

Also, for the last session of the story I have used past future tense. Writing it drove me nuts. I have tried to minimize the errors, but I am sure that there will be many more mistakes in the writing. Please feel free to point it out.

I hope you all enjoy the story.

Chemistry Crush a Love Story

I was a very demanding student during my school days when I was preparing for the JEE. I couldn't stand substandard teachers, fearing their ineptitude would affect my rank in the coveted exams. When it came to coaching, I was particular about the teacher having all their concepts clear so they'd never get stuck in any problem whatsoever. If the teacher wasn't able to solve my doubts, I would leave them right away, without even giving them a warning.

There wasn't a culture of the assembly lines of coaching centres in my hometown during those days. There were individual teachers for individual subjects - Physics, Chemistry, and Mathematics. I'd found really good teachers for Maths and Physics but there was a dearth of a good teacher for Chemistry. I attended chemistry classes from three teachers, but to no benefit, as none of them had the requisite fluency I was looking for. During those days, a new teacher Chauhan Sir had started chemistry classes and a lot of students were joining him. A lot of girls of our class had enrolled into his tuitions. Apparently, he was young and good-looking. Disappointed by all the other Chemistry tutors, I went to attend Chauhan sir's class one day. Before the class, upon getting to know my name, he welcomed me and said, "Acha, so you are Harsh. Ishita takes your name a lot."

Ishita was a new student in our school who joined in the 11th grade. She came from Mt. Carmel, the all-girls school famous for short skirts and fluent speakers of the English language. We had never interacted before, though our roll numbers were adjacent and we were partners in the Chemistry lab. I had a feeble crush on another classmate at that time, but when Chauhan sir mentioned Ishita's name, my previous crush was whitewashed in an ever-growing infatuation for this new girl Ishita. Ishita, who took my name a lot, that's how I started remembering her.

I attended each and every class of Chauhan sir thereafter, even though he turned out to be much worse than every other teacher that I had encountered before, just to catch that one glimpse of the ponytail of Ishita. She always sat on the front row designated for girls, and I, on the last, safe and far away from her so she could never catch me checking her pony. Being the wimp that I was, we never talked in class. I nevertheless couldn't keep my eyes off her. Whenever I saw her talking to Chauhan sir, I imagined that it was about me. When the tuition would get over, I would wait for her to leave first and I'd casually walk past her father's Maruti 800 stuck in the traffic, mock-solving equations in the air, hoping she would watch my geekiness and fall for me even more. Why else would she take my name to Chauhan sir if not for my academic brilliance?

Slowly, I became Chauhan sir's most regular student and made sure I outperformed everyone else in his class, topping each of his tests, just to maintain my good impression on Ishita. Though my disappointment with Chauhan sir's limited capability made sure that I scouted for other teachers around, finally finding a tutor who was scholarly, but it didn't make me leave Chauhan Chemistry Centre ever.

Two years later, when I was in IIT, Ishita-my great crush-added me on Facebook. Having lost my wimpy self, I chatted for a while and quizzed her, "Ishita, acha tell me one thing. What would you say to Chauhan sir about me? I am aware you had a crush on me." I anticipated that she would blush, even avoid the topic.

Instead, she instead rebuked me and said, "Hello! You and my crush? Have you seen your face? Stop cooking up these absurd tales, the shitty writer that you are. I was never interested in you."

I couldn't dare to persist and soon enough, perceiving her outright disinterest in me, gave up even though my crush on her didn't. I blamed it on the years that passed since those days. She might have found a new crush, I deduced. Months later, I met a few of my school friends for a reunion. While we were sharing tales from our school, one of them shared how he attended Chauhan sir's classes just because of Ishita, his crush. His crush? That even she liked him.

"You kidding me, bro? Is Ishita really interested in you?" I asked, taking him to the sides, horrified.

"For sure. Though I am yet to confront her about this but," he said. and added, "you know, Chauhan sir had told me the first day I joined his tuitions that Ishita takes my name a lot."

I guffawed, not knowing if the laugh was on him or on myself. At that moment, all I could think of was whom should I ask for my money spent on tuition back from Chauhan sir or my crushed crush Ishita?

Balcony Letter the Comfort ex 166

what seemed like an instant? And then it was time to go. As Aftab stood up to leave, Shikha said, "Wait! I have something that I need you to deliver to someone,

Aftab."And she produced a small package out of her bag. It was a brand-new woman's perfume, wrapped in brown paper with a note that said, "For Aunty."

(Thanks to my dearest friend Farakh Nargis Abbas for sharing this real story of his. It was first published in my book, Green Mango.